ANNA'S SECRET FRIEND

Yoriko Tsutsui

illustrated by

Akiko Hayashi

Anna was excited about moving to a new house in a new town. She was especially pleased to be living close to the mountains. But already she was missing the friends she had left behind.

Still, there was hardly time to think about anything because there were so many boxes to be carried into the new house.

Soon every room was full of boxes. Anna began to help unpack, but before long she was bored and tired.

Suddenly she heard a quiet tip tap sound. The noise came from the front door.

"I heard the postman," said Anna.
"I don't think it could have been," said her mother.
"We haven't told anyone our new address yet," said her father.
"But I *did* hear someone," said Anna, and she went to look.

At the front door Anna saw that her mother and her father were right. There were no letters, but there was something much nicer – a small bunch of violets that lay on the floor. How did the pretty flowers get there?

Quickly Anna opened the front door to see who could have brought the flowers. But all she could see was an unfamiliar street, and lots of people she hadn't seen before walking by.

Next morning Anna's mother did more unpacking.
"I just don't know who could have given those violets to us yesterday," she said to Anna.

Just then, Anna heard that noise again – a quiet tip tap sound at the front door.

Anna ran to the front door. This time there were three dandelions in the letter box. Anna carefully picked out the yellow flowers and opened the front door. But once again all she saw were people she didn't know walking along the street.

The next day Anna went shopping with her mother. It was very strange to be going into new shops and seeing people she didn't know. She wished her old friends were not so far away.

"Just look at those magnificent mountains," said her mother. "I'm sure we're going to love living in this town."

"Who do you think could have left those dandelions yesterday?" Anna asked.

"Maybe they were left for someone who lived in the house before us. Perhaps a little girl's friends don't know she has moved away," answered her mother.

The house was nearly tidy the next day, but Anna's mother was still busy.

Anna drew a picture to send to one of her old friends.

"It's no fun without any friends to play with," she said sadly.

But what was that? Anna heard the same quiet tip tap sound!

Anna rushed to the letter box, and this time she saw a letter in it! There was no name on the envelope, but inside there was a short message written in big letters.

Friends are nice
I'm very happy you have come
I'll be waiting

Anna read the letter again and again.
"I'm sure this letter is for me," she thought.

Anna enjoyed visiting her new school. A friendly teacher showed her all the toys the children played with, and told her about the meadow at the foot of the mountains where the children sometimes played.

"You'll soon make lots of new friends," the teacher told Anna. Anna looked at all the children laughing and chattering in the playground. She hoped that one of them had sent her the letter.

"Violets, dandelions, a letter…
Violets, dandelions, a letter…"
Anna sang as she played marbles by herself.
How she longed for someone to play with!

Just then she heard that sound again — a quiet
little tip tap noise at the front door.

"Wait! Wait!" Anna shouted in her loudest voice as she rushed to the front door. She saw something coming through the letter box! It was a beautiful paper doll.

Anna grabbed the doll and quickly opened the door. She saw a little girl just going out of the gate.

"Wait! Wait!" Anna shouted again.

The little girl turned around slowly. Her cheeks were bright red.

Anna walked down the path.

"Those violets – were they for me?" she asked.

The little girl nodded.

"And … and the letter? Was that for me too?"
Once again the little girl nodded. Anna looked
down at the beautifully folded paper doll in her
hand. All for her! The little girl looked at Anna
shyly and said in a very small voice, "Will you
play with me?"

This time it was Anna who nodded, so both
girls smiled happily and went off to play.

VIKING KESTREL

Penguin Books Ltd, Harmondsworth, Middlesex, England
Viking Penguin Inc., 40 West 23rd Street, New York, New York 10010, U.S.A.
Penguin Books Australia Ltd, Ringwood, Victoria, Australia
Penguin Books Canada Ltd, 2801 John Street, Markham, Ontario, Canada L3R 1B4
Penguin Books (N.Z.) Ltd, 182–190 Wairau Road, Auckland 10, New Zealand

First published by Fukuinkan Shoten, Publishers Inc., Japan in 1986
First published in Viking Kestrel 1987

Text copyright © Yoriko Tsutsui, 1986
Illustrations copyright © Akiko Hayashi, 1986

British Library Cataloguing in Publication Data

Tsutsui, Yoriko
    Anna's secret friend.
    I. Title   II. Hayashi, Akiko
    895.6'35[J]   PZ7

    ISBN 0−670−81670−1

Printed in Japan